Silverlake Fairy School
Dancing Magic

Silverlake Fairy School

A magical world
where fairy dreams come true

Collect the titles in this series:

Unicorn Dreams

Wands and Charms

Ready to Fly

Stardust Surprise

Bugs and Butterflies

Dancing Magic

For more enchanting fairy fun, visit
www.silverlakefairyschool.com

Silverlake Fairy School
Dancing Magic

Elizabeth Lindsay
Illustrated by Anna Currey

USBORNE

For Yumi Star, with much love

First published in 2009 by Usborne Publishing Ltd., Usborne House,
83-85 Saffron Hill, London EC1N 8RT, England.
www.usborne.com

A CIP catalogue record for this book is available from the British Library.

UK ISBN 9780746095331 First published in America in 2012 AE.
American ISBN 9780794530679 JFMAMJJ SOND/11 01563/1
Printed in Dongguan, Guangdong, China.

Contents

Chapter One

Daydream

Mistress Pipit chose two volunteers, Bella and Meggie, from her Charm One Class, to stay behind during break time in order to help clean up the classroom. This left Lila free to say goodbye to her two best friends, flutter down the Swallow staircase, skip from the Hall of Rainbows and run out into the sunshine. Once in the garden, she spread her purple wings and flew to a recently discovered perch high on the castle battlements, where she could look out from Silverlake Fairy

Dancing Magic

School across the waters of Great Silver Lake.

A gusty wind was whipping up the waves but Lila felt not a breath of it. The classrooms of Silverlake Fairy School were warm and dry, and magical charms kept everyone safe. The magnificent silver castle that housed the school stood on its own rocky island. Lila remembered her first glimpse of its mighty walls when she and Meggie had stood together for the first time on the jetty, gazing up at the castle, which had disappeared into the mist. Now, Lila was straining to see the lake's shoreline as swirling gray clouds hid the gaunt crags of the nearest land and the distant Eerie Mountains.

Lila smiled and twirled her glittering, purple wand.

"Outside wintertime; inside summertime," she sighed. "How wonderful fairy magic is. I'm so lucky to be at Silverlake, learning all about it!" She laughed and wedged herself into her chosen

Dancing Magic

perch, keeping well away from the storm raging
out on the lake. Then, with another smile, she
held up the little silver charm that hung from the
bracelet on her right wrist.

"Look, little unicorn," she told the charm. "It's
wild and wintry on the Great Silver Lake. The
waves are galloping white horses. It would be
impossible for a fairy to fly in a wind like that, but
not for the strong unicorn I imagine you to be."

Every fairy studying at the school had a first
day charm, but Lila was the only one who had a
unicorn. She hugged it tight and closed her eyes.

"One day, I'll find out how to make you come
alive," she told it. "I'll magic you into a real
unicorn and together you and I will go galloping."
Lila let her imagination fly with the wind and saw
herself riding as high as the clouds, holding tight
to the unicorn's wild mane, while the wind
threaded knots in her purple hair.

She was so lost in her daydream that it wasn't

until she heard the swish of wings that she opened her eyes. Meggie and Bella had come to get her.

"We were calling and calling you," smiled Meggie. "Didn't you hear the bells?"

"Break's over," said Bella, taking Lila's hand and pulling her from her seat.

"Oh dear, I didn't hear anything," cried Lila, as the three fairies fluttered down toward the Hall of Rainbows.

"Pipity said she's going to tell us about the winter assembly," cried Bella. "And which class is doing the winter show. It might be ours."

"Ours!" said Lila. "But we're only First Years."

They joined the last few stragglers hurrying up the Swallow staircase. The rest of the Charm One fairies were already waiting outside their classroom door, buzzing with excitement. The three friends quickly joined the back of the line.

"Late as usual, you three pathetics," said a pink fairy at the front, before turning sniffily away.

Dancing Magic

Bella, always ready to explode at a jibe, was stopped by Lila's restraining hand on her arm.

"How dare she," Bella spluttered under her breath instead. "We aren't late. We're exactly on time."

"Ignore her," insisted Lila. "This is no time for an argument with Princess Bee Balm." The words were no sooner spoken than Mistress Pipit arrived in a flash of orange wings. The teacher frowned on arguments between her students; it was lucky they had stopped when they did. Smiling, she led the way into the classroom.

Princess Bee Balm's mushroom desk was at the front, close to Mistress Pipit. She sat next to her friend, Sea Holly, a sea-blue fairy with delicate violet wing tips. Bee Balm stared rudely at Lila from under her lashes and then turned innocently to the front to sit on her toadstool and brush her pink gossamer frock into place. Lila hurried to her own desk near the back of the classroom, where

Daydream

Bella sat on one side of her and Meggie on the other, and slid onto her toadstool with a sigh.

Lila's only problem at Silverlake Fairy School was that she was in the same class as Princess Bee Balm. Throughout their time there the Princess had made it clear how much she disliked having Lila, a palace kitchen fairy, at the same school as her high-born royal self. And, with the start of winter coming soon, both fairies would be going home to the Fairy Palace. However, the Princess would go back to the Fairy King and Queen, and Lila to Cook, Mip, the shoeshine elf, and all her other friends in the palace kitchen.

When the class finally settled down, Mistress Pipit sent a hail of tiny orange suns from the tip of her wand and the words *Winter Assembly* appeared magically on the board. Lila listened expectantly to her teacher.

"Now, fairies, there are only four more days left until the end of your first season here at

Dancing Magic

Silverlake Fairy School and a very successful season it's been. Each and every one of you has passed the first Wand Skills Charm Examination. I am very proud of you all. You'll receive your well-earned first Wand Skills Charm at the winter assembly." Mistress Pipit smiled down at the happy faces of her class. "Fairy Godmother Whimbrel has told me that the assembly will take place in the garden, under the stars. And, most exciting of all, my splendid Charm One Class, she has granted you the special honor of putting on the assembly show." The fairies burst into applause. Lila could hardly believe it. When calm was restored Mistress Pipit added, "It's an opportunity for you to show the rest of the school some of the skills you have learned since you joined Silverlake."

Lila almost burst with pride. She could hardly believe that her First Year class had been chosen and that their audience would be the Second, Third, Fourth and Fifth Year fairies as well as all the teachers. It was a scary responsibility, but what a perfect way to end their first season at Silverlake.

"We must invent some stupendous transformation charms," said Lila.

"And have a whizzy fairy dance," added Bella.

"With a magical song," said Meggie. "And I could make the costumes."

Mistress Pipit held up her wand for silence. "Listen carefully. You'll work in your clan groups, Stars, Suns, Clouds and Moons and your Head of Clan fairies have volunteered to help you. Starting tomorrow you'll only have morning lessons in order to give you time to rehearse. You'll meet with your Head of Clan fairies after school today. I'm going to give you time now to discuss and list your ideas ready for those meetings."

"Bats' umbrellas!" said Bella. "This is going to be the best assembly ever."

"Come on, Stars, let's get thinking," said Lila. Cowslip, Periwinkle and Primrose squeezed in and the six Star fairies in the class, sharing three toadstools, sat together in a giggling group.

"There's so much we can do," said Bella, her excitement bubbling and infectious. "We'll make Musk Mallow really proud of us."

Musk Mallow was the Star's Head of Clan fairy and the rest of the Clan really looked up to her because she was also the school's Deputy Head Fairy.

"We'll be the greatest Star Clan team ever, don't you think?" said Lila. The fairies chorused agreement. "All Stars together!"

From the corner of her eye Lila caught Princess Bee Balm sneering at them.

"What a horrible squawking noise the Stars are making! Typical vulgar Pots-and-Pans behavior," said Princess Bee Balm as loudly as she dared.

I don't care what Bee Balm thinks, Lila told herself, *she's not going to stop me from enjoying the show*.

Daydream

"Fairies, fairies, please," called out Mistress Pipit, smiling. "I know it's a thrilling project but I asked you to *talk* about ideas not *shout* about them. And don't forget to write everything down," she added.

"I've got an idea," burst out Bella.

"Shush," said Lila, taking out her scroll ready to write it down. "Whisper."

Princess Bee Balm gave the Star Clan group another irritated glare. Throughout the rest of their discussions Lila kept her voice low and tried not to give anything away. She guessed that whatever the Stars or the Clouds or the Moons did, Princess Bee Balm would want the Suns to produce a bigger, better and more extravagant show.

"You know," declared Lila, thoughtfully, "whatever happens, we Stars must create something brilliantly, burstingly, wonderfully full of starlight."

"Starlight?" said Meggie. "The perfect opposite of sunlight!"

"That is exactly it!" said Lila, smiling at the glowing faces turned rapturously toward her. "It would be just wonderful to make lots and lots of starlight!"

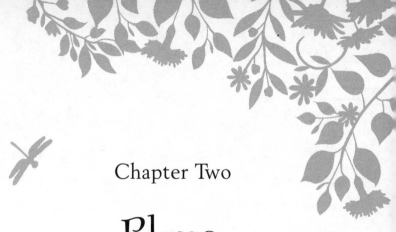

Chapter Two

Plans

After class, Lila, Bella and Meggie found themselves falling a little behind the other Star fairies, who had fluttered on ahead. Meanwhile Bee Balm came flouncing down the Swallow staircase behind them, arm in arm with Sea Holly, while the rest of the Sun Clan fairies followed respectfully.

"Out of the way, Pots-and-Pans, let the Suns through," cried Bee Balm, shoving Lila aside with incredible rudeness. "Oh, and by the way," she said, stopping for a moment, "don't think that twiddly little Stars like you can compete with the golden power of the Suns. We are going to be stupendously the best!" And she continued her parade across the Hall of Rainbows and up the Owl staircase.

"Of all the nerve," said Meggie. Lila stared after the Princess open mouthed, then suddenly burst out laughing.

"What's so funny?" asked Bella. "I so badly wanted to transform her into a slimy slug that I'm amazed I didn't. She is the pits."

"Don't you dare transform her into anything, especially not a slug. It would mean serious trouble," grinned Lila. "Remember the school rule, a fairy must never use her wand against another fairy." Then Lila was overcome by another bout of giggles. "It's just that Bee Balm is…is so predictably horrible!"

"And big headed!" suggested Bella. "And stuck

Plans

up and a bat's umbrella!"

"Yes, all of those things, too," chuckled Lila.

"I wish I *had* turned her into a slug."

"Oh, Bella, be careful," said Lila. "It's not worth letting Bee Balm get under your skin."

"I agree with Lila," added Meggie. "Bee Balm is simply not worth it."

"No, and I don't suppose she'll have time to plan anything underhand," said Bella. "She'll be too busy practicing magnificence."

"We hope," said Meggie.

"Oh, come on, Meggie," said Bella. "What can she do in front of the whole school?"

"Just think of some of the nasty things Bee Balm's done in the past."

"Don't worry, Meggie," said Lila. "We've learned to watch out for ourselves. Come on, the others will be waiting for us and, if we don't hurry we'll be late for our meeting."

The three friends burst into the Star Clan

turret and found Cowslip, Periwinkle and Primrose in the common room waiting for Musk Mallow, a beautiful midnight-blue fairy, who was talking to her friend, Day Lily, the school's Head Fairy. The six First Years arranged themselves in a circle and Musk Mallow joined them. She smiled down at their excited faces.

"We haven't had a season assembly in the garden for a long time," she said. "And neither have the First Years done an assembly show since..." and she thought about it for a while. Across the room Day Lily laughed, her yellow hair turning golden in a sunbeam that had strayed in through the window.

"Since *we* were First Years, Musk Mallow," Day Lily said. "Don't you remember how nervous we were? It was such a great event for us."

"That's right, it was," agreed Musk Mallow. "And we thought the older fairies in the school would be bored watching First Years. We believed they were much smarter than us."

"But you are," said Meggie. "And I'm feeling very nervous."

"Listen," Musk Mallow continued. "Fairy Godmother Whimbrel believes that we should all show each other what we can do from the First Years to the Fifth Years, to build confidence and self-belief, and that way we learn to value every fairy from the youngest to the oldest. All the other classes will give you their full attention, I can promise you that."

"What did you do for your show?" asked Bella.

"We sang, we danced and created a splendid transformation charm, I seem to remember."

"That's exactly what we want to do," said Lila, taking out her scroll.

"Lila's written down our ideas," said Periwinkle, clasping her hands around her knees and shaking strands of lavender hair from her eyes.

"Go on then," said Musk Mallow, turning

smiling eyes on Lila. "Read us what you've written."

Lila tapped her scroll with her wand and it unrolled. From underneath the heading *Ideas for Winter Assembly Show* Lila began to read, "*1. – Amazing transformation charm*, only we don't know what it's to be yet! *2. – Magical Star Song. 3. – Magical Star Dance. 4. – Amazing Costumes. 5. – A good beginning, a fantastic middle and a spectacular end*. That's all I've written down so far, because we couldn't decide exactly what the good beginning and the fantastic middle would be but the spectacular end is going to be our transformation charm."

"And I had an idea for that," said Bella. "Transform the fountain in the Bewitching Pool. Turn the mermaid, the dolphin and the frog into three giant stars and make the conch shell spray teensy-tiny stars instead of water. But everyone said that would be too difficult."

Dancing Magic

"It's a little advanced, I agree," said Musk Mallow, with a flicker of a grin. "Even I wouldn't attempt that."

"But we can look like stars," said Meggie. "Star costumes would be almost as good and I would dearly love to make them."

"Yes, yes," cried the others.

"Are you sure you have time for such complicated costumes, Meggie?" asked Musk Mallow.

"I'll help," said Primrose. "I'm like Meggie, I love making things."

"There, with Primrose's help, it'll be fine. I've been practicing sewing charms for ages." Meggie looked at her silver first day charm hanging from her school bracelet. "And I'll keep trying to make my scissor charm come to life. Magic scissors would really help."

Lila picked up her pencil, sure that Meggie and Primrose would make perfect costumes, and wrote their names next to *Costumes* on her list.

Plans

"I know," said Periwinkle. "We could have clouds that rain stars. That would be really pretty."

"The Cloud Clan might not like us doing that, though," said Cowslip.

"Yes, it's probably best to leave clouds to them," said Musk Mallow.

"We could start with our song and dance," said Lila. "If we were dancing stars we could do spins and make whirlpools of starlight."

"Yes," they all cried. "Yes, yes, yes." Bella fluttered to the ceiling and somersaulted sideways several times.

"Spins are easy-peasy," she cried, dropping to the ground again. "Only they make you dizzy."

"Practice will help you get over that," said Musk Mallow. "Now you'll need some words for your song and I can help you find some music if you like."

"Yes, please, Musk Mallow," they cried.

"Are you going to perform a dance you've

learned this season?"

"Something new," said Bella.

"Yes, the dance must be a special one," said Cowslip.

"Something to surprise Pipity," said Lila. "With floaty music full of long notes to make everyone imagine stars drifting in a night sky."

"I'll see what I can find," said Musk Mallow. "So, to recap, you need a music charm, dance steps, and song words. And your dance will depict whirling, spinning stars. Are you getting all this down, Lila?"

"Oh, yes," said Lila, looking up. "And we'll have our spectacular transformation charm at the end."

"Any other ideas for that?" asked Musk Mallow. Six blank faces stared up at her. "Thinking caps on. You need to have some clue as to what this can be by tomorrow's rehearsal. I'm going to the library now to find you some music. I'll be back later to see how you're doing."

Plans

"Thank you, Musk Mallow," they called after her.

"We know we're going to have a song and a dance," said Lila. "But the end of the show is the most important part of all, the part you build up to, the part that has to be the best."

"The climax," said Meggie.

"Exactly," said Lila.

The six fairies furrowed their brows trying to come up with an idea. "It needs to be something simple but spectacular," Lila went on. "And we need the idea soon or we'll have no time to practice and make the transformation charm perfect."

Chapter Three

Argument

The fairies sat and thought; they walked around the room and thought, and Lila doodled on her scroll and thought. Then Bella yawned and stretched and everyone turned expectantly toward her.

"Why are you all looking at me?" she asked.

"We thought you'd had an idea," said Lila.

"'Fraid not. Bats' wings, thinking is tiring. Maybe I'll go to bed and dream one." Bella paused. "Wait a minute, Lila, you could do a dream wish.

x

Argument

Why didn't we think of that before?"

"No, I couldn't," said Lila, dashing the hopes of the other five fairies. "I don't want to do a dream wish in public. I may be getting better at them but they take a lot of concentration and don't always last as long as I want them to."

"Oh, forget dream wishes. Wouldn't it be wonderful if you could make your first day charm come alive, Lila?" said Periwinkle. "You'd be the first fairy in our class to discover how to do it and a real live unicorn would be a perfect end to our show."

"Well," said Meggie. "We'd all like to do that and, let's face it, every one of us has been trying to do it ever since we got our charms."

"Yes," agreed Bella. "Don't hold out your hopes, Periwinkle. There are plenty of Fifth Years who've never managed it let alone us First Years. I think it's pretty unlikely to happen."

"I keep trying when I remember," said Lila.

"It's just that there are so many other things to do as well."

"Anyway, how does a unicorn fit in with our theme?" Bella asked.

"He could gallop to the stars," said Primrose. "Or pull stars around the sky or something. Oh, I don't know," she finished lamely.

"Fairy Godmother Whimbrel said my unicorn might come to life if I can find out his name," said Lila. "She told me to tap it with my wand when I've found the right one." The unicorn swung backward and forward on her bracelet. "From now on, I'll keep trying," Lila promised. "Anyway, let's not get distracted. If we can't think of the perfect transformation idea tonight, we absolutely must by tomorrow."

"That's right," agreed Bella. "Otherwise we'll look really stupid if the other clans have come up with a good idea and we haven't."

Lila went to bed, her head full of thoughts.

Argument

They had a beginning idea, a middle idea but still no dramatic end to their show and they only had three days to find and rehearse one. As she snuggled down to ponder the problem, she was sure that Bella and Meggie were doing the same. She could hear them tossing and turning under the sheets.

The stars twinkled brightly through the open window and Lila held up her wrist to look again at the tiny silver charm on her bracelet. She had made lists of possible names, all of which had turned out to be useless so far. It was a problem that had vexed her on and off for the whole time she had been at school. No, the unicorn could not be counted on to come to life. There was a much better chance that one of them would dream the perfect transformation ending as Bella had suggested. But when Lila awoke the next morning, her mind was as blank as it had been the previous night and she couldn't remember dreaming anything at all.

At breakfast in the refectory, over plates of scrambled dandelion petals and cashew nut cream on toast, the six Star Clan fairies clustered around one side of the Charm One table. The Sun Clan fairies were having their own meeting on the other side.

"Dream anything interesting, anyone?" Bella asked hopefully, after swallowing her last mouthful of breakfast. She looked from one glum fairy face to another. "Neither did I," she muttered. "Not a single acorn sausage of an idea."

"Something dramatic, something explosive, something truly magical," said Cowslip, as though she had been repeating those words to herself all night.

"Wait a minute," said Lila. "Cowslip's right. What could be better than finishing with something explosive…a huge dramatic whoosh?"

"A great big something!" said Bella, her

Argument

eyes lighting up. "A great big…?"

"Shooting star!" Lila finished. "It can go round and round above the audience and flood the garden with magical light."

"Yes," cried the other Star fairies triumphantly.

"Problem solved," cried Bella.

"No," came a cry from across the table and Princess Bee Balm leaped to her feet. "You've just stolen our best idea!"

"We haven't," protested Lila. "I just thought of it this minute."

"Exactly! You've been listening in, haven't you Pots-and-Pans. *Flood the garden with magical light* – that's our dramatic ending. You're not doing the same thing as us. We thought of it first."

Sea Holly took hold of Bee Balm's arm but was roughly shaken off. Bee Balm was scary when she was angry and even the Sun Clan fairies looked shaken.

Dancing Magic

"We'll have what we like," said Bella, leaping into the fray. "And you can have what you like. Nobody's stolen your idea."

"And why can't the Suns and Stars both make magical light?" Lila asked. "It's certain to be a different kind."

"Not different enough," stomped the furious Princess.

"But a shooting star can never be the same as a glowing sun or whatever you've planned," Lila said.

"I agree," said Bella. "There is a difference."

"Sunshine is different from…" and Lila pondered briefly. "From starshine!" The new word popped into her head from nowhere and she loved it instantly. The unicorn on her bracelet trembled.

"One's daylight and one's night light," added Periwinkle, helpfully.

"And they both fill the garden with magical

Argument

light," said Bee Balm ominously. "It's my idea and you unimaginative, mud-brained Stars can't use it."

"We can if we want to," said Lila, really irritated. "Starshine is different from sunshine."

"And I'm telling you, Lilac Blossom, you can't use it," said the Princess ominously.

"You think what you say goes," said Lila, getting more and more cross by the second. "But it doesn't. You are a bumptious balloon of a princess filled up with your own importance." Lila's cheeks flamed purple and the little unicorn on her bracelet jiggled up and down. If she had been paying attention, which she hadn't been, she'd have realized it had been doing so for some while. Was it warning her to stop? Lila was too angry to care. "We can't always be kowtowing to you just because you're royalty. If we want to light up the garden with magical starshine, we'll light up the garden with magical starshine." The unicorn

Argument

jumped up and down but Lila had no intention of stopping now. Besides she liked this new word "starshine" that had just popped into her head. It was a great invention.

"You tell her, Lila," urged Bella.

"How *dare* you speak to me like that!" said Bee Balm, eyes blazing. "You're forgetting where you come from, you, you floor washer, you…you pots-and-pans scraper, you lower than a worm, purple pimple."

"What's wrong with washing floors? And what's wrong with being purple? It may be a rare coloring but at least I share it with Fairy Godmother Whimbrel."

"Oh, well said, Lila," grinned Bella. "Couldn't have put it better myself."

The Princess was taken aback. She had clearly forgotten that Lila and their Headteacher were the same color.

"Oh, go sink in the lake!" she hissed.

Dancing Magic

"You think you're better than everyone in the whole school, Bee Balm, but let me tell you, you're not. You're always putting on airs and graces and I'm fed up with it. A real princess would care about her subjects but not you; you only care about yourself."

Enough, Lila thought quickly, putting her hand over her mouth before she said something that would make the situation even worse. As it was, the whole table of First Year fairies was staring at her, and Bee Balm's eyes were glinting with venom.

"And you can't stop us from using our own idea," said Bella continuing by herself.

"Oh, can't I?" said Bee Balm, her face pale and dangerous. "You just wait and see."

Before the argument could escalate any further there was a flutter of wings and Musk Mallow arrived with Marigold, the Head of the Sun Clan.

Argument

"What's all the shouting about?" Musk Mallow asked.

"The Stars have stolen our idea," said Bee Balm.

"That is so not true," said Bella. "Lila thought of the magical light idea just now, all by herself."

"Oh, for goodness' sake, Bee Balm, you haven't started another argument?" said Marigold. "If this is true, you're making a disgraceful scene about nothing. The show is exactly that – a show – not a competition. If both teams want to make magical light, that's absolutely fine."

"Yes, she did start the fight as usual," said Bella.

"That's enough, Harebell," said Musk Mallow. "If there are going to be a lot of silly arguments the show will end up being canceled." They were saved from a further telling-off by the bells ringing for the start of lessons. "We'll discuss this later, Stars." Musk Mallow's eyes rested on Bella. Bella stomped crossly from the refectory with Meggie fluttering after her.

"Sorry, Musk Mallow," said Lila. She glanced toward the Princess and received a chilling look. Lila made a quick decision and hurried out to join the rest of the Stars. She caught up with Bella and Meggie in the Hall of Rainbows and took hold of Bella's arm.

"Bella, we can't have Bee Balm against us again," Lila said earnestly. "We've got to rethink this. It's not just us this time, remember, it's all the Stars." Primrose, Cowslip and Periwinkle hurried to join them and Bella glanced at their troubled faces.

"That argument with Bee Balm was bad enough. We don't want another one," Lila finished.

"I agree," said Musk Mallow, coming up behind them. "I'm sure you can find a more unusual ending than a shooting star. Something that will be more unexpected."

Argument

"What can be more of a surprise than a shooting star?" said Bella. "We can't let Bee Balm ruin our display. It's what she always does. And a shooting star is the best and most dramatic ending in the world."

"Was," said Lila firmly. "We are going to think of something else."

Chapter Four

First Rehearsal

Lila was distracted all through morning lessons. Bee Balm kept shooting poisonous glances over her shoulder toward the Star fairies at the back of the class. Lila understood why Bella was upset about having to give up the shooting star idea. She was upset herself. It was easy to imagine the transformation of something humble, like a pebble, into a beautiful five-pointed star that would launch itself across the garden, leaving a sparkling trail of tiny stars, before exploding into

First Rehearsal

an inky sky and filling the garden with magical light. But they couldn't and maybe Musk Mallow was right, a shooting star from the Star Clan was perhaps a little obvious. Cupping her chin in her hands, Lila stared out of the window. If only she could think of something else!

"Lilac Blossom!" Mistress Pipit said. "Have you finished?"

"Oh, no, sorry, Mistress Pipit," said Lila, blushing a deep purple. She quickly picked up her quill and looked down at her scroll. She was supposed to be drawing a pretty green-and-white-topped mushroom called a polka dot. But her thoughts kept slipping back to the troubling question of the show ending.

The rest of the lesson dragged slowly by and it was a relief when Mistress Pipit finally said, "Quills down." At least now Lila could think without feeling guilty.

"Listen carefully, everyone," Mistress Pipit said.

Dancing Magic

"Your show rehearsals start this afternoon. I want you all to come back to the classroom after lunch to receive some instructions first. Please, don't be late."

The bells rang and it was time to go. The class picked up their wands and filed from the room. The moment they were outside the door Lila said, "Quickly, quickly, Stars! A meeting!" And she led the way down the Swallow staircase and out into the garden.

"Do you have a new idea for the ending?" Primrose asked when they were all outside.

"Not exactly," said Lila. "But I've been thinking about what Musk Mallow said: we need something that will be more unexpected than a shooting star."

"I agree," said Meggie.

"Yes, a shooting star from the Stars, well, that does seem a little obvious," added Periwinkle.

"That's all very well," said Bella. "But until

someone comes up with a better idea it's the only one we've got."

"We will," said Lila, sounding more certain than she felt. "There are six of us. One of us will think of something." Lila tapped her wand against her knee. "And I'm sorry I said what I said to Bee Balm now. Getting cross with her is always a terrible mistake. And Marigold told her off in front of everyone. The Princess is not going to forget that in a hurry."

During lunch in the refectory, Lila was rather subdued. Bee Balm kept throwing her sinister and threatening glances whenever their eyes met. She was certain the Princess was hatching some dastardly plan to avenge her wounded pride and wondered what it might be.

But, by the time the fairies were gathered together in the classroom, Lila was feeling more optimistic and soon became infected with the excitement of the rest of the class, even though Princess Bee Balm kept looking in her direction, then pointedly turning away.

Mistress Pipit raised her wand ready to speak: "I've agreed rehearsal spaces with your Head of Clan fairies," she said. "The Clouds and the Moons wish to do their show together and will practice in the Bugs and Butterflies ring so they have plenty of space. The Suns will rehearse in the garden by the Bewitching Pool and the Stars in the Flutter Tower. I will be coming around to see how you're doing and will be available to help you with your costumes. Any questions?" There were none. "Then off you go."

Lila got halfway to the door but had to go back for her scroll. The moment Mistress Pipit was out of earshot Bee Balm started complaining to the Suns.

"That is typical. The Stars get to rehearse in the

First Rehearsal

Flutter Tower – the very best place of all. Well, they may think everything's going their way but let me tell you it's not."

"If you want to rehearse in the Flutter Tower, I'm sure the others wouldn't mind switching. Or we could take turns," Lila suggested, thinking this a good opportunity to make peace.

"Eavesdropper! How dare you listen in on a private conversaton," hissed the Princess. "I wouldn't share anything with you and your pathetic copycat Star friends, ever."

"We're not copying you and anyway we've given up on the shooting star idea. We're doing something much more original than concentrating on magical light."

And without waiting for a reply Lila hurried from the classroom.

"About time too," said Bella when she joined the others in the garden. "I was about to come and find you."

Dancing Magic

"I've told Bee Balm we've given up on the shooting star idea and that we've got something more original that we're going to do," Lila said. "Now we've got to think of something fast or we're going to look really silly."

"Well done," said Meggie. "Maybe she won't go around looking so sour now she's heard that."

"You wish," said Bella. "She's not going to forget Lila's words in a hurry."

"Don't remind me," said Lila.

But she soon forgot about Bee Balm. The Star fairies were smiling and eager to get going, especially Bella. And the blue and red leather-bound book that Musk Mallow was carrying under her arm aroused Lila's curiosity.

"Follow me," Musk Mallow said, fluttering into the air. The Star fairies rose up behind her in a colorful cloud of yellows, blues and Lila's deep purple. Their wings became transparent in the sunlight as they flew up high over the Wishing

Dancing Magic

Wood toward the top of the silver tower that stood at its center.

Lila always loved being in the Flutter Tower. It was a wonderful fairy gymnasium where the class had practiced for the school Flying Proficiency Test. Fairy dance and fairy gym had become two of Lila's favorite lessons and both took place in there. The fairies fluttered down from the opening in the roof to the floor and Musk Mallow carefully laid down the blue and red book on a gossamer cloth.

Fairy Song and Dance Through the Ages, Lila read. She was impressed. Fancy Mistress Hawthorn allowing Musk Mallow to take such a precious volume from the library. The librarian was the strictest mistress in the school and all the Charm One fairies were scared of her.

"I chose this particular book because it has the most useful dance steps," began Musk Mallow.

"Does it have any music charms?" Bella asked.

First Rehearsal

"Oh, yes, lots," said Musk Mallow, opening the book at a page she had marked. "But I want you to think about dance steps first, and I've found these movement diagrams to give you some ideas."

"I can see a twirl that we can do," said Lila. "Arms high and toes pointed."

"That's the corkscrew," said Musk Mallow. "It's not the easiest step to do on the ground, but during flight it can be very effective – although it does need a lot of wing control." Lila made up her mind to try that. "And don't forget your star theme," Musk Mallow added.

"Here's a star step," said Bella. "It turns the body into a star shape. We could try that."

Meggie studied the star step intently.

"Hmm, this will work well with the costumes I've been thinking of," she said.

Musk Mallow turned to the next page.

"Oh, look at that wonderful spinning circle we could make," said Cowslip. "It looks really pretty."

Dancing Magic

Musk Mallow turned another page and the chattering and exclaiming increased. There were so many diagrams in the book; somersaults and dives, swoops and backflips.

"Can we try out some dance steps?" Primrose asked.

"Of course," said Musk Mallow. "Put your wands somewhere safe. This is your chance to experiment," she smiled, raising her own wand. "I've found a music charm that I hope you'll like. I want you to try out lots of different movements."

Musk Mallow waved her wand and a drift of midnight blue smoke rose from its star tip. The music began with several long fluting notes. It reminded Lila of twinkling stars and the slow glide of a pale moon arching its way across a velvet sky. It was a haunting melody and just perfect.

Lila twirled upward, following the lazy spiral made by the smoke, stretching her arms up and her legs down and keeping her toes pointed. She experimented with some swoops and somersaults and the corkscrew spin. It wasn't her most graceful step but she managed to land without falling over as the final notes faded away.

"Well done, everyone," said Musk Mallow. "I'm impressed. You created some delightful dance movements." She closed the book. "I don't think we're going to need this anymore. There are some very imaginative fairy dancers here." The six Star fairies glowed with the praise. But that didn't mean Musk Mallow wasn't going to make them work very hard. By the time the session drew to a close they had learned at least eight useful new dance steps.

"But the thing is," said Lila, "we've still got the words for our song to write. Meggie and Primrose need to make the costumes…"

"Cowslip and I can write the words for the song," said Periwinkle. "And if you could teach us the music charm, Musk Mallow, we can fit the words to the music tonight."

"There we are then," cried Bella. "We're done."

"Not quite," said Lila, looking down at her scroll with a frown. "There's just a little matter of the finale, the climax to our show, our grand transformation charm. What are we going to do for that?"

"Lila why don't you and Bella go and sit quietly in the library for a while and think about it?" suggested Musk Mallow. "Meggie and Primrose can make a start on the costumes while I teach Cowslip and Periwinkle the music charm. I'll meet you all in the common room after dinner to see how you're doing. Off you go and good luck!"

Lila, Bella, Meggie and Primrose arrived back in the Hall of Rainbows to start on their tasks. Meggie and Primrose set off to find Mistress Pipit for sewing supplies.

First Rehearsal

"Well, they're all right then," said Bella, watching the fairies trip up the Swallow staircase. "They know what they're doing."

"Let's do what Musk Mallow suggested and go to the library to think," sighed Lila.

"Why is sorting out what should be the most dramatic part of our show so difficult?" grumbled Bella, as Lila towed her through the Hall of Rainbows. "And why do we have to do our thinking in the library? You know how scary old Thorny is. We get into trouble practically every time we go in there."

"But this is where the books are," said Lila. "They might give us an idea." And without more ado, Lila lifted the heavy latch on the library door and pushed her unwilling friend inside.

Chapter Five

The Lost Wand

The moment the door closed behind them Mistress Hawthorn looked up from her desk and peered at the new arrivals over her spectacles. Both fairies curtsied politely. The librarian gave them a nod and they hurried to find a free table.

Lila led the way between some bookshelves into an alcove, slipped her wand into her waistband and put down her scroll on the vacant table.

"We'll look for a transformation book first. That will give us ideas," Lila whispered.

The Lost Wand

"Good thinking," Bella whispered back and, looking more cheerful, she plonked her wand next to Lila's scroll. "There are millions of books in here. There must be one that can help us."

Bookshelves ran all the way around the great library and up the walls to the ceiling. There were steps to climb and galleries to reach, but where should they begin?

"What are you looking for?" The voice, coming from so close, made them both jump.

"A transformation charm," said Lila, hardly risking more than a glance up at the librarian, who had followed them over.

"A special one," added Bella, more boldly. "For the show."

"Oh, I know what it's for," said Mistress Hawthorn, almost but not quite smiling. "You're not the only Charm One fairies who've been needing my help. Follow me."

Lila turned to see Bee Balm and Sea Holly

watching them from a table covered with open books. Their hostile stares gave her an uncomfortable feeling. *I hope they're not up to mischief*, she thought. *Searching out some wicked charm to try out on me.* She caught up with Mistress Hawthorn by a shelf labeled *Transformation*.

"I particularly recommend *Celebration Charms for Beginners* and *Transformation Charms for Festivities*," the librarian told them. "I hope you find what you want." And leaving them to it, she returned to her desk.

"Bee Balm and Sea Holly are over there," whispered Lila, uneasily.

"I saw them," said Bella. "I guess they're working on their Sun charm, whatever it is, thingy," said Bella.

"Yes, well, they didn't look too pleased to see us," said Lila heaving out *Transformation Charms for Festivities*.

"Oh, this book's no good," she said, quickly

turning pages. "It's about making statues and fountains."

"And this one's about making cakes or decorations and other completely useless stuff," sighed Bella.

They put the two heavy books back on the shelf and kept looking.

"We need our transformation to look wonderful under the stars," said Bella.

"Yes, a night sky full of twinkling starshine," said Lila.

Her silver unicorn gave an unexpected jump. She turned to see the Princess coming toward them carrying a small book.

"Oh, uh, hello, Bee Balm," said Lila, awkwardly.

"Your Royal Highness, to you, Pots-and-Pans," said the Princess.

"Your Royal Snobfulness, you mean," said Bella. "In case you've forgotten dear, delightful, and oh-so-charming Princess Bee Balm, let me remind you, you're supposed to be treated the same way as everyone else when you're at this school."

Bee Balm ignored Bella and put the book back on the shelf, flicking back her shiny pink locks.

"Hurry up, Sea Holly," she said as her friend arrived staggering under the weight of the rest of the books. Bee Balm looked down her nose at Bella and then turned to Lila. "I've nothing more to say to you, Pots-and-Pans, except that I forgive your insulting words as a noble princess should and I warn you that nothing will beat the magnificence of our rising sun. Whatever you Stars try will fail. Believe me, you don't stand a chance."

"And what's that supposed to mean?" said Lila.

"Take it to mean whatever you like," answered Bee Balm with a smirk. "Got you worried now, have I?"

"We're not worried by a pinky-ponk like you," said Bella.

The Lost Wand

"What did you call me?"

"A pinky-ponk or should it be a pinky-stinky!" said Bella sniffing the air dramatically.

"Bella!" said Lila, shocked. "Don't!"

"Well, she asked for it. Taking another dig at you like that."

"Please, let's not sink to her level," said Lila.

"You're right," said Bella. "Bee Balm's level is such a long way to fall, we might hurt ourselves." Lila struggled to keep a straight face.

Bee Balm and Sea Holly exchanged annoyed glances and the Princess walked off with her nose in the air. Sea Holly hastily crammed her pile of books on the shelf and hurried after her. A library elf came tut-tutting over to put them back in the right order.

"Her – *forgive your insults*, I don't think so, Lila," muttered Bella as she watched the Princess and Sea Holly sit down at their table again and begin writing furiously in their scrolls.

Dancing Magic

"You're right about that. Bee Balm never forgives anything," said Lila, picking up a slim red and gold volume at the end of the shelf. "I'd love to know what exactly it is she's planning but I suppose we'll find out soon enough."

"You bet we will," said Bella. "Bats' umbrellas, she makes me sick."

Lila turned the pages of the slim volume, which had the intriguing title, *Transformation Charms in the Big Top*.

But, by the time they had looked all the way through the book, they were no closer to finding what they wanted. Lila gazed steadily at the last picture as if hoping for inspiration. It was of a circus big top. A banner flew from the tallest tent pole displaying the words, *Manfredo Mantollini's Traveling Circus*. It was a very long banner as it had a lot of words to fit in.

"I feel like running away and joining Manfredo Mantollini and his traveling circus," said Bella. "It

The Lost Wand

would be more fun than this. There's absolutely nothing useful in any of the books we've looked in and my head is one big blank."

"I feel the same," said Lila, wrinkling her brow. "Bella, why don't you go and see if you can help Meggie and Cowslip with the costumes? There's no point in both of us getting nowhere."

"Good idea," said Bella, perking up at once.

"I'm going to keep thinking," said Lila. "But not in here. Sitting that close to Bee Balm and Sea Holly is distracting me." Lila put the circus book back on the shelf and followed Bella to the door.

Mistress Hawthorne glanced at them over her spectacles and the two fairies bobbed a curtsy and hurried out.

"I think I'll go up to the battlements," Lila said once they were safely in the Hall of Rainbows. "That's a good thinking spot."

"Just get a great idea," Bella said. "You can do it. See you later," and she hurried off up the Owl staircase to find the rest of the Stars.

Lila noticed that Bee Balm and Sea Holly had followed her out of the library so she quickly took herself into the garden and wasted no time in fluttering up to her perch. She made herself comfy by tucking her scroll in to her waistband. Then, folding her arms around her wand, she gazed out at the Great Silver Lake.

If anything the water was rougher than it had been the day before. The wind had whipped up great waves and Captain Klop's little boat was bobbing like a cork alongside the jetty. And there was the dragon gatekeeper, standing on the drawbridge that linked the jetty to the castle, raising a great claw to shield his eyes from the sun that was pouring through a newly found gap in the brooding clouds.

The dazzling sunlight reminded Lila of why she was sitting there and, particularly, of why a rising sun transformation charm would be magnificent. What, oh, what could the Stars do to end their display?

The wind moaned around the turrets, but although Lila could hear it she couldn't feel it. The gusting came and went lifting spray from the huge waves that pounded against the castle wall far below.

"Manfredo Mantollini's Traveling Circus," Lila recited. "Manfredo Mantollini's Traveling Circus." It had a certain jolly rhythm. "Manfredo Mantollini's Traveling Circus." Then, from nowhere, an idea popped into her head. It was the very one. "Yes," she cried to the little unicorn charm. "Yes, yes, yes!" And the unicorn jumped on her wrist. She saw a flash of pink and felt unexpected hands on her back. The shove that followed was impossible to avoid; she couldn't stop herself. Her wand went in one direction; she in the other. Both tumbled over the wall.

Try though she did, it was impossible to fly in

the gusty wind. Down Lila went, buffeted over and over, until she hit the water with a stinging splash. The cold was terrible. She struggled not to gasp; not to breathe. Down she went, sinking lower and lower into the chill waters, her purple hair lost in a swirl of bubbles. It seemed to take forever before she could kick and push upward, but at last, desperately holding her breath, she began a slow rise through the green water toward the surface. But she was a long way down. Maybe too far down. Soon she was going to have to breathe. She was. *Hang on*, she told herself, *hang on*.

The light above dimmed; more bubbles, a shadow. A large, dark shape loomed above her. Something strong gripped her around the waist. Powerful wings beat the water and the dark shape carried her toward the light.

Lila came into the air spluttering and gasping. A wave slapped her face but she didn't care. She was safe.

Dancing Magic

"I've got you, little Lilac Blossom." She held tight to the arm that encircled her and looked up into Captain Klop's worn dragon face. "Lucky I saw you fall. A little fairy like you could have been swept anywhere in this gale." He held her firmly against his scaly chest while his strong, wet wings beat the wind at its own game and carried them firmly toward the jetty. He didn't mention that she might have drowned, but Lila knew how close she had come to it.

The dragon landed and put the trembling Lila down on firm stone.

"Thank you, Captain Klop, thank you," Lila gasped, still holding tight to his arm. She turned back to the waves, her voice quavering. "Something terrible's h...happened. I've l...l...lost my wand! What am I g...g...going to do?" Cold and unhappy Lila burst into tears. It felt as though a part of her was missing. She had lost her power to do magic. What was going to happen to her now?

Chapter Six

Lila's Idea

Captain Klop gave Lila his large white handkerchief to wipe her eyes and rub her hair dry and insisted she told him exactly what had happened.

"You sure you was pushed?" he asked. "It's not the kind of thing a fairy would do."

There is one fairy who might, Lila thought and bit her lip.

"The fairies in this school be a caring, responsible bunch," Captain Klop continued. "If someone did push you they put you in terrible danger."

"Yes," said Lila, thinking, *I was pushed and pushed hard*. She shivered more violently, realizing how dangerous Princess Bee Balm could be.

The kindly dragon walked her across the drawbridge and through the gateway. Lila was grateful for the comforting tingle of her bracelet as it allowed her back into school. *At least I still have my little unicorn charm*, she thought.

"You know what you've got to do now?" said the kindly dragon, his eyes gentle in spite of his fierce-looking face with its torn ear and broken tooth.

"Go and tell Mistress Pipit what I've done?" said Lila, dreading having to report her lost wand. She had loved it; it had been her perfect wand, presented to her at her first school assembly, its purple had perfectly matched her hair color and its magic had always worked beautifully for her. Now it was lost, goodness knows where, in the

Lila's Idea

choppy waters of the lake, and with the show such a short time away, she wouldn't have a chance to look for it. What was Mistress Pipit going to say?

"Want me to come with you?" Captain Klop asked.

"No, no, I feel braver now," said Lila, trying to smile.

"You was always brave, little Lilac Blossom," said the dragon. "Cook told me so and Cook be right."

"You've rescued me from the water twice now, Captain Klop," said Lila. "Once, when I was a tiny baby, floating in the basket on the Ocean of Diamond Waters, when you gave me to Cook, and now, from the stormy waters of the Great Silver Lake."

"So I have, little fairy," nodded the dragon. "So I have." And Lila put her arms around his neck and kissed his scaly cheek. "Now, that's enough

Lila's Idea

of that soppy nonsense," he said, softly pushing her away. "Off you go." But his twinkling eyes told Lila he was pleased.

Some while later a dismal Lila arrived in the busy Star Clan common room after an uncomfortable interview with Mistress Pipit. Periwinkle and Primrose were singing, silver gossamer fabric was stretched over the chairs and cardboard was spread across the floor. Meggie was snipping, and Primrose was measuring and Bella was gluing. It was a veritable hive of activity.

"Lila!" said Meggie, looking up with a pleased smile. "How did it go?"

"Well…" Lila began.

"Your wand's a different color!" At these astonishing words Primrose halted the music and everyone came over.

"What's happened to it?" Bella asked.

"It's a borrowed wand. I've lost mine," Lila told them.

"What?" said Bella, horrified. At once, each fairy wanted to know the when and the how and the why, and Lila told them as best she could.

"But what did Pipity say?" Bella asked.

"She was really nice about it considering," replied Lila. "You see I didn't tell her that I was pushed off the battlements, I said I slid off."

"Oh, Lila," said Meggie.

"Well, I did slide off. Now Pipity has banned me from sitting there and I guess everyone else will be too from now on."

"Why didn't you tell her you were pushed?" said Bella.

"Because I didn't see who it was, not for certain and, if it was Bee Balm, I don't want her to be expelled."

"Why ever not?" said Cowslip. "She deserves to be."

"Because, oh it's too complicated to explain

now," said Lila. "I would hate her to blame me for it, that's all."

"But do you really think it was Bee Balm?" Meggie asked.

"Of course it was her," said Bella. "Which other fairy would be so...so irresponsible and stupid? And after all she said about forgiving you."

"Look, I provoked her, which makes me partly to blame."

"That's ridiculous, Lila," said Periwinkle. "You told her the truth and whatever you may have said Bee Balm had no excuse to put you in danger. You might have drowned."

"Not Lila," said Bella. "She swims like a fish."

Lila didn't like to contradict Bella or admit how near the truth Periwinkle's words were; she didn't want to worry her friends.

"That's not the point," insisted Periwinkle.

"Well anyway, at least Pipity's loaned me this,"

said Lila, holding up the rather worn green wand. "I've got to pay for a new one. Cook's not going to be pleased. It's going to cost two golden sempireans." One fairy sempirean was more money than Lila had ever had in her whole life, let alone two.

"Wow," said Bella. "That's a lot!"

"I'll have to work really hard over the vacation to make up for it," said Lila. "It's the only thing I can do."

"But isn't there a charm she could do to get it back for you?" Periwinkle asked.

"There must be," said Bella.

Lila shrugged. "If there is she didn't suggest it."

"She thinks you lost it by being careless," said Meggie. "She wants to make you feel responsible, I guess."

"Typical teacher," said Bella in disgust.

"Anyway," said Meggie, giving Lila a hug, "before

the horrible part happened, tell us, did you have any ideas?"

"Oh, yes," said Lila, some of the shine returning to her eyes. "I had a really good one. Can I borrow a tiny piece of that silver fabric, Meggie?"

While a sliver was cut for her, Lila darted into her bedroom and came back with an empty inkwell.

"Watch," she said, squashing the fabric inside the inkwell and placing it on the floor. "It should be no more difficult than the transformation charms we practiced for our Wand Skills Exam."

"Won't the fabric get inky?" asked Bella.

"It doesn't matter if it does," said Lila. "By the time I've transformed it, it'll be something quite different."

Periwinkle gave Bella a knowing wink.

"Just checking," said Bella, wryly.

Lila pointed the green wand at the inkwell and gave it a flick. "Silky silver banner!" she said.

Dancing Magic

A few tiny green stars half-heartedly dropped to the floor, missing the inkwell completely. "Oh, butterburs and bodkins, this wand is useless."

"Wait a minute," said Meggie. "Let me try a color charm on it. The wand should work better if it's the same color as you." With a quick flick of her own wand Meggie sprayed yellow-ocher stars over the green wand. Gradually it changed to a deep purple.

Meggie smiled. "Wow, it worked. I've never tried a color charm on a wand before."

"You are so smart, Meggie. Thank you. It feels better already. Okay, here we go. Silver silky banner," Lila cried. This time a puff of purple stars fell onto the inkwell.

"But nothing's happened," said Bella.

"That's the clever part," said Lila. Reaching into the inkwell with her fingertips she took to the air. As she fluttered higher, a sparkling silver banner streamed from the inkwell. Lila flew

Lila's Idea

twice around the common room before the end finally came free, but it still wasn't long enough for her.

"Bother, the wand should have made the banner much longer than this but, with everyone else joining in on the charm, I guess it will be. See, the banner's as light as a feather and really strong. Now all Bella and I have to do is figure out a charm for the words Star Dance Extravaganza. It'll be written in diamond stars. It's going to look wonderful. Imagine it, all six of us pulling a great sparkling banner across the night sky."

"Oh, Lila," said Meggie. "Star Dance Extravaganza, what a wonderful title for our show. It'll make magnificent starshine."

Lila's unicorn gave a little leap but she was too busy unraveling herself from the banner and grinning about Meggie's use of her newly invented word "starshine" to notice.

"I bet nobody's ever done a banner before,"

said Bella. "It'll be unique and original."

"Then when we come to earth again we undo the charm and the silky banner will go back into the inkwell," said Lila.

"Why don't Primrose and I turn the inkwell silver?" suggested Meggie.

"Oh, yes," said Bella. "Won't it be wonderful when such a huge long banner comes out of a boring little inkwell! We must keep the ending a secret and make it a big surprise."

"It's going to be the best fun ever," said Periwinkle.

"And it's so simple to do," said Lila. "Is everyone happy with that idea?"

"Yes," the five fairies chorused back at her, laughing gleefully.

"So we've just got to figure out how to do the words," Lila said, eager to get the charm just right. She jumped up. "Come on, Bella, we have one day to make this charm work perfectly."

Lila's Idea

"Well, I'm ready," said Bella.

"Then let's get on with it."

Chapter Seven

Winter Assembly

The following morning the Star fairies gathered in the common room before breakfast. Lila was excited but frustrated. She had been the only fairy in her class to get a distinction in the Wand Skills Examination but with the borrowed wand getting a straightforward charm to work was almost impossible. Neither she nor Bella could magic the letters *Star Dance Extravaganza* correctly onto the banner. They kept appearing in the wrong order and disappearing again.

Winter Assembly

"It's odd, isn't it?" said Bella. "I should be able to make the charm work with *my* wand even if your borrowed one is useless."

"Not necessarily," said Lila. "Creating the banner is the easy part. But we've never tried writing on anything before. Still, six wands together will be much more powerful."

"We must practice together to make sure," said Bella.

"But, we're doing really well apart from the transformation charm," said Periwinkle. "We've written the song, worked out the dance and the costumes are nearly finished. All we need to do now is make sure we know everything. That's the hard part, remembering the moves and the words with so little time to rehearse." The bells for breakfast rang as she was speaking.

"Bring your scrolls to the refectory, everyone," said Lila. "We must make sure we know exactly what we're doing." She wished she felt more confident at this late stage and was really missing her own wand.

At breakfast the Charm One table was buzzing with activity. Clouds, Suns, Moons and Stars were gathered in clan groups around the table, eating heather honey porridge, hazelnut crunchies and brushing crumbs from their scrolls. Lila ignored Bee Balm but the Princess finally caught her eye and said gloatingly, "I hear you've lost your wand, Pots-and-Pans. Your transformation charm won't be so spectacular now, will it? Not with a borrowed wand. Poor you!"

This sent a stir of surprise among most of the other First Year fairies. The Stars had been careful to tell no one else what had happened. Lila and Bella exchanged meaningful looks. So how did Bee Balm know? Meggie squeezed Lila's hand. Periwinkle, Primrose and Cowslip also understood the implication of the Princess's words. It made Lila even more certain that it was Bee Balm who had pushed her from the battlements.

The Princess didn't gloat for long. She was tense and tempers were fraying at her side of the table. Perhaps the rising sun charm was more difficult than the Princess had imagined. Not that Lila cared. Right now she had her own problems and was determined that the lost wand would not get in the way of a really good transformation charm to end the Stars' show. She was going to work her hardest to make it perfect, whatever it took. They had a long afternoon of rehearsals ahead of them.

By the time they arrived back in the Star Clan turret that night, the Star fairies were exhausted. They had tried on their costumes, sung the song over and over and danced until they could dance no more. Lila fell into bed with a grateful sigh.

"It was a good day," she said sleepily to Meggie and Bella.

"But we still aren't getting all the letters of

the transformation charm right even when we do it together," said Bella.

"We will tomorrow," sighed Lila, suddenly confident after a mostly successful rehearsal. "It'll be entirely perfect tomorrow."

However, when Lila woke up the next morning she was far less optimistic about the banner lettering. Today was the actual day of the assembly. Time was tight and she felt decidedly jittery.

"Wake up, Bella," Lila said, giving her friend a shake. "It's time to get up."

She found Meggie already at work with Primrose in the common room, putting the finishing touches to the star costumes. Bella joined them, a little bleary eyed.

"Now, Bella, concentrate," said Lila, "this time we're going to get the words right."

Lila was looking around for the inkwell when Meggie said, "Wait a minute, you two." And she handed it to them covered in a silver sheen and glittering delightfully. "Sorry it's taken so long but there's been so much to do."

"That's great, Meggie," said Lila. "Thank you." And she pushed the sliver of fabric inside. To avoid the older Star fairies seeing their rehearsal, Lila and Bella went back into their bedroom.

Lila put the inkwell on the floor and both fairies pointed their wands. After a delicate flick they said in unison, "Write *Star Dance Extravaganza* onto our silver banner!"

Lila took hold of the end and pulled. Out streamed the banner and she and Bella flew it around and around the bedroom in circles. This time the letters read, *Tras Dnace Zaextraganva* and some of the letters were upside down as well. Bella groaned.

"Let's not bother with the letters if they won't come out right," she said. "It's pointless."

Lila stared thoughtfully at the inkwell.

Dancing Magic

"Bella, why don't you try it by yourself?"

"Me?" said Bella. "You're much better at transformation charms than me."

"Please, try," said Lila. "Just once."

Bella pointed and flicked her wand, then said, "Write Star Dance Extravaganza onto our silver banner!"

Lila pulled the banner from the inkwell and spread it out around the bedroom. The words were faint but, this time correctly spelled – *Star Dance Extravaganza*. "Well would you believe it?" said Bella, astonished.

"It's this wand," said Lila. "It's ruining everything. I'll have to work without it." She flung it on her bed in disgust. "Actually, five wands will be plenty. I should have realized that before."

The rest of the day flew by. During morning lessons the class spent time with Mistress Pipit in the garden, deciding on the best place to perform. In the end, they chose in front of the Bewitching

Winter Assembly

Pool. Then after lunch, while the older fairies, with the help of Captain Klop, began constructing a stage, Musk Mallow took the Star fairies to the Flutter Tower for a final run-through.

The six fairies took their places and began. The song and the dance went smoothly, except when Primrose fluttered the wrong way, and Meggie almost spun into Bella, but those mistakes were quickly corrected. When they picked up their wands for the transformation charm, Musk Mallow held up her wand.

"Okay, stop there," she grinned. "I want the charm to be my surprise tonight. I know it's going to be good, so now I'm going to leave you to it." And Musk Mallow did just that.

"Well?" Bella whispered to Lila.

"Five wands," said Lila. "I'm not going to ruin everything with that borrowed wand. I'll do the display without it."

"Won't that look a little odd?" asked Bella.

Dancing Magic

"You could just carry it."

"I'm taking no chances," said Lila. "It's not going anywhere near our transformation charm and if necessary I'll have to explain to Pipity."

Since early morning, Lila had carried the little silver inkwell with her everywhere. They had hardly seen Princess Bee Balm all day but even so, Lila was too edgy to take any chances. The rest of their free time before the show was spent trying on their costumes in the Star Clan turret, which was fun.

By the time the sun had dropped behind the castle walls and the shadows had lengthened, the excitement was growing. The five fairy classes sat on the grass in front of the stage, their wands lit up so that the stars, moons, suns and clouds at the tips shone brightly.

Lila's eyes darted everywhere – the garden looked the most magical she had ever seen it, especially when Mistress Pipit charmed the lights from hundreds of fireflies. Lila was so excited she could hardly sit still.

Applause broke out when Fairy Godmother Whimbrel arrived on the stage in a cloud of purple and silver stars. Everyone stood up and clapped until their hands tingled. Smiling at the welcome, the Headteacher held up her wand for silence and gestured that they should sit down again.

"First, I want to congratulate every single fairy at Silverlake Fairy School for your hard work so far. You have all passed your examinations and I am now going to present you with your hard-earned charms. We'll begin with Mistress Pipit's class, Charm One."

One by one, fairies fluttered up onto the stage and curtsied. Fairy Godmother Whimbrel tapped each school bracelet with the star at the tip of her wand. Under a burst of tiny purple stars a first Wand Skills charm was soon hanging from each of the First Years' school bracelets. When Bella received her charm her face split into the widest of smiles. Bella may have failed all her charm exams last year, but she had certainly made up for it now. Lila was really proud of her.

"Look how pleased you are now," Lila whispered in Bella's ear. "It was worth all that hard work, wasn't it?" Then after Meggie had received her charm it was Lila's turn. She fluttered onto the stage and curtsied.

"Well done, Lilac Blossom," said Fairy Godmother Whimbrel, tapping Lila's bracelet. "You've earned your distinction with real hard work." Lila was entranced to see her second charm hanging close to her little silver unicorn.

"It's a pretty charm too," whispered Lila to her friends when she was sitting down again. "There's a W, an S, a D and a one, entwined together."

"That's your D for distinction, clever you," Meggie whispered. "Which is why it's such a pity that you've lost your wand and can't take part in our transformation charm properly."

Dancing Magic

"Well, at least I've managed a decent idea," said Lila, trying to make the best of it.

By the time all the charms had been given out a crescent moon hung in an inky sky. *It's a perfect banner-flying night*, thought Lila, gazing up at the twinkling stars.

"And now, Charm One will end our assembly with their show," announced Fairy Godmother Whimbrel. "And while the First Years are getting ready the Fairy Glee Club will sing the Flutter Fair Song. Up you come, Glee Club, and off you go and get ready, Charm One."

Lila's class flew to the far side of the Bewitching Pool to put on their costumes. Bee Balm made sure her Sun fairies were far away from the Stars, but Lila still kept a wary eye on her.

"My tummy's full of butterflies," said Meggie, as she helped Lila into her costume. The star fit perfectly over Lila's wings, leaving them free to flutter.

Winter Assembly

Then Lila helped Bella with her costume. It looked wonderful.

"Oh help!" cried Cowslip. "The Moon and Cloud fairies are almost ready to begin."

"Put your wands down, move well away from them and stand in a circle, everyone," instructed Meggie, then she and Primrose held up their wands and shook golden-yellow stars over all six fairies, turning hair, wings and frocks to silver.

"Wonderful," smiled Primrose.

"We're not going to charm the wands in case we upset their magic," said Meggie.

"But please, can you wrap these silver ribbons around them instead?" asked Primrose.

"Have you got the inkwell, Lila?" Bella asked, nervously.

"Yes," said Lila, tapping her pocket. "It's in here."

They put out their wand lights. Now all they had to do was wait.

Dancing Magic

"No wand, Lilac Blossom?" said Princess Bee Balm sidling over. "Borrowed one no good? What a shame."

"Shut up, Bee Balm, we know what you did," said Bella, before Lila could stop her.

"Me?" replied Bee Balm, laughing. "I didn't do anything, did I, Sea Holly?"

"Of course you didn't," said Sea Holly and both fairies burst into giggles.

The harmonious sound of singing voices died away as the Flutter Fair Song came to an end and, when the applause was over, Fairy Godmother Whimbrel went back onstage.

"I believe the Charm One fairies are now ready," the Headteacher announced. "For the first part of our show we have the Moon and Cloud fairies: Daisy, Larkspur, Sweet Pea, Peony, Chrysanthemum, Milkwort, Candytuft, Snowdrop, Pansy, Poppy, Clover and Hyssop in *Storm*." There was an encouraging round of applause and, as the audience put out their wand lights, the fireflies dimmed leaving the garden in shadow.

"Isn't the starshine beautiful?" Lila whispered in Meggie's ear. Immediately, Lila's unicorn charm gave a huge leap and her whole arm tingled. She was so surprised that she didn't hear Meggie's reply. Her fingers closed around the little charm and she instinctively looked around for Bee Balm. Where was she and what was the unicorn trying to warn her about? Lila swallowed nervously, every sense on red alert. She couldn't see a single thing in the gloom. The Moon and Cloud fairies were about to start. She kept checking the waiting shadows of the Sun fairies yet somehow managed to concentrate on the stage as well. It wouldn't be long before it was the turn of the Star fairies and she really didn't want anything to go wrong.

Chapter Eight

Star Dance Extravaganza

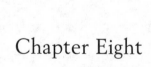

The Cloud and Moon fairies fluttered into the air weaving beautifully timed dance movements with their music; flying above the audience, they transformed a saucer into a moon and cotton balls into clouds. The newly made moon hung above the garden, bathing the audience in silver-yellow light, while the music grew louder and fiercer. The fairies danced between scudding storm clouds that hid, then revealed, the glowing moon, making a kaleidoscope of shadows and moonbeams. When the music faded away, the moon was transformed back into a plate and the clouds into cotton balls, as the Cloud and Moon fairies dropped onto the stage and curtsied. The Star fairies clapped as loudly as the rest of the school. Lila thought the Cloud and Moon part of the show was wonderful. The delighted performers fluttered from the stage, and Lila knew the other two parts had a lot to live up to.

"And now we have *Dance of the Fires* performed by Bee Balm, Sea Holly, Coral Flower, Fuchsia, Figwort and Cynthia, the Sun fairies," Fairy Godmother Whimbrel announced.

"Watch and learn," said the Princess, coming deliberately close to the Star fairies and giving Lila a dig with her elbow. "You'll never beat this." Lila rubbed the spot, then held tight to her unicorn. At least if Bee Balm was performing she couldn't be getting into any mischief.

The music began and the Sun fairies twirled and

whirled in their flame costumes. As she watched, Lila's thoughts drifted back to the battlements, when she had listened to the bluster of the wind on the lake. That sound must have drowned out Bee Balm's wingbeats. If only she hadn't let go of her wand. If only. Where was it now? Deep under water or washed up on some far distant shore?

The furious music gradually became calmer and the Sun fairies dropped entrancingly to earth, no longer flames but glowing embers. Then one of the fairies lifted up an orange ball. At this signal the others rose, fluttering, into the air. With a wave of their wands the ball glowed brighter and brighter and grew bigger and bigger. Using their wands, the fairies guided the glowing ball, sending it higher and higher into the sky.

As a ripple of appreciation ran through the audience, Lila felt a tap on her shoulder and turned to find Candytuft holding out a purple wand. Lila's heart almost bounded from her chest.

Star Dance Extravaganza

Candytuft put a finger to her lips and whispered, "Captain Klop said it's yours. He found it floating on the lake."

Lila clasped the wand tightly and gave Candytuft the hug she longed to give Captain Klop. She felt so elated she could hardly stand still. But she had to and, grinning like anything, she forced herself to concentrate. She joined in with everyone else as they gazed at the glowing sun. It lit up the faces of the fairy audience and turned night back into day.

Then, unexpectedly, Sea Holly sneezed, her wand wobbled, the sun tilted and the other fairies scattered, ignoring Bee Balm's furious commands to stay where they were. The golden sun dropped from on high and splashed into the Bewitching Pool, narrowly missing the mermaid statue's conch shell. A glowing orange ball bobbed to the surface, hissed and went out. Cheers and applause burst from the audience.

"But honestly, that's not how it was supposed to happen at all," cried Bee Balm, trying to explain. "The sun was supposed to go over the battlements and land in the lake. It was your fault, Sea Holly, you ruined everything."

When the Stars discovered that Lila was holding her own wand it gave them a real boost of confidence.

"Watch and learn," said Bella, impishly, when Bee Balm went by.

"Oh, you've got it back!" Bee Balm exclaimed, unable to disguise her annoyance when she caught sight of the wand.

"Yes and it's no thanks to you, Bee Balm," said Bella.

"Go fall flat on your faces," Bee Balm snapped, flouncing off.

The Star Clan fairies hurried onstage. Lila carefully placed the silver inkwell in the center of the platform, having checked one final time that the sliver of fabric was safely inside. Then they stood ready.

"Good luck, everyone," Lila whispered, her mouth a little dry and her heart beating at twice its normal speed.

"And to end our show we have the Star fairies, Lilac Blossom, Primrose, Harebell, Cowslip, Nutmeg and Periwinkle," announced Fairy Godmother Whimbrel.

"Ready?" whispered Periwinkle.

"Yes," the others whispered back.

Three beribboned wands and one purple one – Lila had had no time to decorate it – were placed on the ground, pointing toward the inkwell. Lila, Bella, Meggie and Primrose hurried into line as they had rehearsed, their silver star costumes glittering as merrily as the real stars in the sky. With a flick of their wands, Periwinkle and Cowslip began the music charm and hurried to join the waiting line.

Dancing Magic

As the first fluting notes trilled across the garden the fairies fluttered into the air. Tiny silver stars sprayed from the star points on their costumes. *How talented Meggie is*, Lila thought, as she heard a sigh of appreciation from the audience. The fairies began to sing:

From star to star
Star to star
Fluttering hither
Fluttering thither
High so high
In a glittering sky…

They were flying level with the battlements now, their clear fairy voices echoing around the castle turrets; busy wings keeping them nicely steady.

We are star fairies
Watch us fly…

Dancing Magic

They repeated the song and thousands of tiny stars cascaded onto the stage in a waterfall of dazzling brilliance before going out. The audience gave them a round of applause.

Now the Stars began to dance, stretching elegant arms and shaping their legs as Mistress Pipit had taught them, first with spins – three to the left and three to the right – before they fluttered into position on their backs, holding their knees to their chests. They stayed in this position, hard though it was on their wings, and looped the loop in giant spins and swooping somersaults, spraying stars as far as the Wishing Wood. Lila could hear gasps from the audience and knew it must look amazing from the ground.

Next they broke ranks and with graceful darting movements, fluttered hither and fluttered thither, to remind the audience of the words in the song. Sending star sprays in chaotic directions they finally raised their arms, pointed their toes and, keeping beautifully together, corkscrewed back down to the stage, leaving a trail of stars to catch up to them. With applause ringing in their ears they ran to pick up their wands ready for the transformation charm.

Lila nodded and they all pointed star tips at the little silver inkwell. With her own wand back in her hand Lila felt supremely confident, until, from the corner of her eye, she saw Bee Balm in the shadows making several sudden sharp wand movements. What was she doing?

"If only there was more starshine I could see," Lila muttered desperately. Her unicorn obviously agreed. It leaped around urgently on her bracelet. She could hear it tinkling against her Wand Skills charm as though trying to attract her attention.

The Princess was definitely pointing her wand in their direction. She wouldn't use it against them, would she? By now Lila was extremely agitated. Together, the Stars recited, "Write *Star*

Dancing Magic

Dance Extravaganza onto our silver banner," and pointed their wands at the inkwell. There was a yelp and somebody's wand shot skyward with a rocket-like whoosh. The power of take off was truly astounding. Everyone watched the wand vanish high into the night sky. There was lots of applause.

"Who's wand was that?" Lila asked under her breath.

"Mine," groaned Bella. "It just shot itself into the air."

"Don't move, anyone," said Lila. "The audience doesn't know something's gone wrong." Bee Balm was doubled up with silent laughter and Sea Holly was smirking behind her. "Listen, we'll pull the banner out as we planned and go after the wand at the same time. When it starts to fall it'll glitter in the starshine."

Lila didn't get a chance to tell Bella not to worry because her unicorn jumped so wildly then it hurt. Bee Balm had done one dastardly deed, was she about to do another? It didn't look like it; she was still collapsed with the giggles.

"Starshine?" Lila said again, holding up her bracelet. "Starshine!" And without thinking she touched the unicorn charm with the tip of her wand. There was a purple explosion and a gasp from the audience, who, as one, took in a deep breath and held it.

A real live silver-white unicorn pranced across the stage toward Lila; his mane and tail a rippling purple.

"Your name, oh, what a discovery, your name – it's Starshine!" Lila held out her hand and touched the unicorn's velvety nose. In reply he blew softly onto her fingertips. "Hello, Starshine," she whispered.

Chapter Nine

Starshine

The silence in the garden was so intense it felt as though the watching fairies were caught in some extraordinary spell. All eyes were on Lila and the unicorn. Even Bee Balm stood frozen. Only Fairy Godmother Whimbrel sat gently nodding, a wise smile on her lips as though this was what she had been expecting all along. Lila gently stroked the unicorn's warm neck.

"Please, Starshine, will you help me bring back Bella's wand?" The unicorn dropped his beautiful

Starshine

head and Lila quickly reached into the inkwell for the end of the banner. Pulling it out behind her she fluttered fearlessly onto Starshine's back. "Meet me on the battlements, friends. Starshine and I are going to get Bella's wand." And, as if this was his command, the unicorn sprang into the air. A glittering cavalcade swept up into the night sky, Lila and the unicorn trailing the banner, the other Star fairies, their costumes spraying yet more silver stars, fluttering to the battlements, leaving the audience applauding and Bee Balm a picture of fury and envious dismay.

"Starshine the speedy," Lila cried as the wind rushed by. Up and over the castle wall flew the unicorn, up and up he galloped, the banner a great silver tail sweeping the sky behind him. There was only water beneath them now. And above them the wand was spinning and twisting toward the lake. Closer and closer it came but not quite close enough. Lila, at full stretch, missed it and the wand continued its fall. The unicorn turned, galloping at such terrifying speed that it took all Lila's concentration to hang on. The wand was only seconds away from splashing into the water but Starshine caught up with it.

"Whoopee, I've got it," Lila cried triumphantly. "Starshine, I've got it." Cheers came from the watching Star fairies on the castle wall. "Upward, Starshine, we've got a show to finish!"

The unicorn galloped to the top of the wall and waited by the battlements for a few seconds, giving Lila time to hand back Bella's wand and for the five Star fairies to take hold of the banner.

"Here we go," cried Lila, twining a handful of purple mane around her fingers. "Hold tight, everyone."

Then with the banner flapping wildly and the cries of the five exhilarated fairies behind him, Starshine galloped back into Silverlake Fairy School. The unicorn flew them around the Star

Dancing Magic

turret, across the Wishing Wood and twice around the Flutter Tower, while the words *Star Dance Extravaganza* trailed in a rippling, steady stream above the wildly applauding audience.

Never in all Lila's life had she experienced anything like this. Her wildest dreams had been realized; her handsome, magical unicorn had come to life. "Starshine, Starshine, Starshine," she said over and over again into his ear. The unicorn tossed his head, his golden horn aflame, carrying a rider who couldn't stop smiling.

But even such a dramatic flight had to end. Lila's class had been fantastic and she hoped that Mistress Pipit was as pleased as she was. The unicorn cantered from the sky and trotted across the stage in front of the wildly cheering audience. The Star fairies let go of the banner and, with a wand tap, it fluttered back into the silver inkwell. Jumping from the unicorn Lila put her arms around his neck.

Starshine

"Thank you, Starshine," she whispered. "Thank you very, very much."

"Well," said Bella, breathless and grinning. "I've changed my mind about Bee Balm. She can charm my wand again whenever she likes. Thanks to her, I've just had the best time of my whole life."

Mistress Pipit was all smiles, insisting that her Charm One Class line up and take a bow. Starshine took center stage and, bending one knee, he lowered his graceful head – another magical moment. Fairy Godmother Whimbrel applauded as enthusiastically as everyone else and Lila almost burst with the thrill of it; she could bring her little charm to life at last.

Fairy Godmother Whimbrel joined Mistress Pipit and the Charm One fairies on the stage, raising her wand as she did so and, while the cheers slowly died away, she put an arm around Lila.

"Well done, Lilac Blossom," she said. "I'm more than proud of you." Lila blushed purple to the roots of her hair. She caught sight of Captain Klop in the shadows and beamed. The old dragon nodded his head in a satisfied way and Lila knew that he was as pleased as she was.

Meanwhile, Bee Balm's face was one big scowl. It didn't bode well for life at the palace, but right now Lila didn't care. She was not going to let the Princess spoil this moment. "I'd like to say a big thank you to our Charm One fairies for a truly dramatic display," Fairy Godmother Whimbrel told the school. "Our First Year fairies are bursting with talent as they have so ably proved tonight, not that I doubted it for one minute." She smiled warmly. "Thank you very much, Charm One, to each and every fairy." She let her eyes rest on Bee Balm briefly. Bee Balm looked down and blushed.

"Three cheers for Fairy Godmother Whimbrel and Mistress Pipit," cried Bella. "Hip-hip hooray!"

After the cheers and applause faded away Fairy Godmother Whimbrel raised her wand one

Starshine

final time and announced that there were refreshments ready in the refectory. Lila looked up at the Headteacher longing for one more gallop.

"It's time to send Starshine back to your bracelet, Lilac Blossom," said Fairy Godmother Whimbrel gently. "He's young like you and, like you, he needs a rest. It's been an exciting day. Tap his golden horn with your wand and he'll be gone."

"Thank you, Starshine, thank you for everything," said Lila curtsying to him. She must remember that. He's young like me. Starshine gave a unicorn bow and whickered, nudging Lila's hand in a friendly way with his nose. The golden horn on his forehead glinted and then he shook himself all over. Lila stroked his silky neck and slid her arm over his withers.

She didn't want to say goodbye, but she knew she had to. She raised her wand. Starshine lowered his head. Tap! And he vanished in a hail of purple stars. Now there were two silver charms on her bracelet once again. Tears welled in Lila's eyes at the sudden loss until she remembered that he was going to come alive for her again and again and again. He was her very own unicorn.

"I think I'm the luckiest fairy alive," she whispered to Fairy Godmother Whimbrel.

"Maybe you are," smiled Fairy Godmother Whimbrel. "You're certainly a very special young fairy."

"And I've met Starshine before, you know. I first saw him after I'd been swimming in the river one morning near to the Fairy Palace. Does that mean he always knew he would be mine? Even before I knew I was coming to this school?"

"That is a mystery I can't explain," replied Fairy Godmother Whimbrel. "All I can tell you is that some fairies have the rare gift of drawing a unicorn to them."

Starshine

"Oh," said Lila, feeling suddenly humble. "I can hardly believe I'm one of them. Me? I'm just a kitchen fairy."

"Nobody is *just a kitchen fairy*, Lila, remember that," said Fairy Godmother Whimbrel. "Now, let's go in, it's time for some refreshments and then bed." Fairy Godmother Whimbrel put an arm around Lila's shoulders and gently steered her toward the Hall of Rainbows.

Later, when she was tucked up but too excited to sleep Lila thought about everything that had happened over the past few days.

"You won't be lonely on my bracelet anymore, little unicorn, not now you've got my Wand Skills charm next to you," she told Starshine sleepily. "And I have only to whisper your name, tap you with my wand and you'll come to life again. But I won't now because Musk Mallow's made me promise to wait until tomorrow. That's when I'm taking you home."

Dancing Magic

Lila snuggled down and began to think about how much she was longing to see Cook and Mip, the shoeshine elf, and all her other friends in the palace kitchen. "And I won't have to *tell* everyone about you, Starshine – I can *show* them." She gave the tiny silver charm a kiss and, with a long satisfied sigh, fell fast asleep.

Join Lila and her friends
for more magical adventures at

Silverlake
Fairy School

www.silverlakefairyschool.com

Unicorn Dreams

Lila longs to go to Silverlake Fairy School to learn
about wands, charms and fairy magic – but
spoiled Princess Bee Balm is set on ruining Lila's
chances! Luckily nothing can stop Lila
from following her dreams...

Wands and Charms

It's Lila's first day at Silverlake Fairy School, and she's
delighted to receive her first fairy charm and her own
wand. But Lila quickly ends up breaking the school
rules when bossy Princess Bee Balm gets her into
trouble. Could Lila's school days be numbered...?

Ready to Fly

Lila and her friends love learning to fly at Silverlake
Fairy School. Their lessons in the Flutter Tower are a
little scary but fantastic fun. Then someone plays a
trick on Lila and she's grounded. Only Princess Bee
Balm would be so mean. But how can Lila prove it?

Stardust Surprise

Stardust is the most magical element in the
fairy world. Although the fairies are allowed to
experiment with it in lessons, stardust is so powerful
that they are forbidden to use it by themselves.
But Princess Bee Balm will stop at nothing
to boost her magic...

Bugs and Butterflies

Bugs and Butterflies is the magical game played
at Silverlake Fairy School. Lila dreams of being
picked to play for her clan's team, and she has
a good chance too, until someone starts cheating.
Princess Bee Balm is also being unusually friendly
to Lila...so what's going on?

About the Author

Elizabeth Lindsay trained as a drama teacher before becoming a puppeteer on children's television. Elizabeth has published over thirty books, as well as writing numerous radio and television scripts including episodes of *The Hoobs*. Elizabeth dreams up adventures for Lilac Blossom from her attic in Gloucestershire, where she enjoys fairytale views down to the River Severn valley. If Elizabeth could go to Silverlake Fairy School, she would like a silver wand with a star at its tip, as she'd hope to be with Lila in the Star Clan. Like Lila, Elizabeth's favorite color is purple.